To _____

Love _____

First Candlewick Press hardcover edition 2003
First published in Great Britain in 1991 by Walker Books Ltd., London.

The Library of Congress has cataloged the paperback edition as follows:

Butterworth, Nick.
My grandpa is amazing / Nick Butterworth. — 1st U.S. ed.
Summary: A child describes an amazing grandfather.
ISBN 1-56402-099-1 (paperback)
[1. Grandfathers — Fiction.] I. Title.
PZ7.B98225Myf   1992
[E] — dc20   91-58746
ISBN 0-7636-2057-2 (hardcover)

2 4 6 8 10 9 7 5 3 1

Printed in Hong Kong

This book was typeset in New Century Schoolbook.
The illustrations were done in watercolor.

Candlewick Press
2067 Massachusetts Avenue
Cambridge, Massachusetts 02140

visit us at www.candlewick.com

My Grandpa is
AMAZING

Nick Butterworth

CANDLEWICK PRESS
CAMBRIDGE, MASSACHUSETTS

My grandpa is amazing.

He builds fantastic
sand castles . . .

and he makes
exotic drinks . . .

and he's not at all
afraid of heights . . .

and he makes beautiful
flower arrangements . . .

and he's an excellent
driver . . .

and he knows
all about first aid . . .

and he's got
a great motorcycle . . .

and he's a terrific
dancer . . .

and he's very, very,
very patient . . .

and he invents
wonderful games.

It's great to have a
grandpa like mine.

He's amazing!